THE CONIUM REVIEW

vol. 5

Conium Press
Portland, OR

The Conium Review
Vol. 5
© 2016 Conium Press
Portland, OR

http://www.coniumreview.com

ISBN-10 1-942387-09-1
ISBN-13 978-1-942387-09-1
ISSN 2164-6252

Cover Image: © Brilt / Adobe Stock
Internal Images: © Brilt / Adobe Stock
Layout & Design: James R. Gapinski and Uma Rallabhandi

THE CONIUM REVIEW
vol. 5

[contents]

[contents]

BIRTH

Jessica Roeder

BIRTH

Jessica Roeder

Each time we give birth, we think it is the last birth for us. We writhe each in her stump house, we are wrung inside and out, we push and push and wait and huff and push. The umbilicus toys with our torn parts until we cut it away. The baby, always a surprise, so much like the last and yet so far from human. So unlike us or the last baby as he is now. We begin to suspect that our babies are taken away. We have a bawling red mass—a limbed thing, certainly, but certainly also a furious unshapely mess. We have pains. We have baby girls, baby boys. Then we have quiet, and our father. We feed him, we wash him at night. We rest when we can. We leave our hair long and lank. We could clothe our babies in our hair alone, we could braid a rope of it if we had scissors, a rope of sister hair, we could loop the rope around our father's neck as he slept. When he is with all of us, he is often sleeping. We could strangle our father, yes, and see if our babies grow. We could walk out through the gravel. We could bury him in rocks.

COPY MACHINE

Samantha Duncan

COPY MACHINE

Samantha Duncan

I've been working as the office copy machine for two weeks, and I already feel more intimately connected to people. The things anyone wants copies of, even in this day and age. It didn't come perfectly, at first, the paper coming out crumpled and unsatisfactory. Online searches revealed this may be due to my acid reflux. I worked around it, though, and can now pull a crisp, flat piece of paper from my mouth with a clear image (luckily, my eyesight is still in good condition) of the original document requested.

My family doesn't understand why I signed up for this, but they mostly don't have the capacity to understand. The actual copy machine breaking isn't a good enough reason for them. Maybe not for me, either. "Be a dreamer," they say. I prefer to wedge my round self into this square hole and see where things go from there.

Being a mirror is a confrontational act. Kyle brings three photos of his cat for me to copy and can't even make eye contact (not that I need eye contact to make the copies, but it is a kind acknowledgment). I can only speculate why he wants photocopied images of his pet in three very common household cat places (the couch, the kitchen counter, the windowsill), but speculation can be a waste of energy. Inquiring is out of the question.

Neil needs seventeen copies of a death certificate. When I give him a questioning look, he says, "It's crazy, man. You have to have one of these for every account they ever had." I'm really just wondering who died. It must be somebody close to him if he's taking care of their affairs, but he never said anything at the morning meeting.

Lori brings magazines from the break room with recipes for delicious, hearty meals. Enchiladas, beef stews, cheesy casseroles. I don't know if any of it gets made. In my four years with the company, I've never once seen her eat. Not at lunch time, not at her desk, not even at the monthly birthday celebrations. It would require a stretching of the imagination to believe she ever goes home and makes these meals, as belief isn't my job, but I copy them for her, nonetheless.

One day, Reagan brings me an Insane Clown Posse CD booklet. I'm speechless. Never would have taken her for a fan. "I just need the logo," she says. I copy it, hand it to her, and spend the rest of the day guessing where on her body it's going to go, because surely she's getting it tattooed. But then, why take a copy to the tattoo artist, instead of the original from the booklet? Maybe she wants it more rugged looking. That's a thing nowadays, right? Or maybe it's not a tattoo at all, maybe it's to hang somewhere. Or for a friend. For what?

I spend half an hour mulling over some possibilities. Mike brings me an invoice to copy, which I do while answering an email to Ellen about our Friday night plans.

"So, what do you make of all those wigs Harriet's been wearing?" Mike says.

"She's trying out new looks, I guess. She's not sick or

anything. I don't think she's taking it seriously. I mean, they all look ridiculous," I say.

"Half the time, she says hi to me in the hall, I don't even recognize her," Mike says, and we laugh in agreement. I hand him his invoice.

Later, an email from Ellen: *Ridiculous? What are you talking about? I don't wear wigs.* I reread my earlier email and realize I transcribed Mike's comments in the middle of finalizing our dinner plans. Need to be more vigilant about that. There can be no multitasking while copying.

More Insane Clown Posse paraphernalia copies for Reagan as the week goes on. So much that on Friday, I feel it almost necessary to ask her what the deal is.

"My brother likes them," she says, collecting the sheets of paper as they emerge from my mouth, her movements so fluid, like we're a figure skating team that's been practicing this for months. "I'm making these collages to send to him while he's in rehab. It's kind of hard to explain. I don't know why you want to know. I haven't really told anybody about it."

"I'm sorry if that was prying too much," I say. She looks regretful and defeated, walks away. I finish some reports, pick two bits of paper out of my left bottom molar. Lori comes by with another cooking magazine, the pages she wants already dog-eared.

"My grandmother used to make this," I say when I flip to the sausage-stuffed pasta shells she wants. "Before she died, that is. It was awful. Too much flavor. I couldn't stand it."

"Well thanks, that really makes me want to make it now," Lori says, snatching the paper out of my mouth and giving me what feels like a paper-cut on the corner where my lips met.

"Damn, I didn't mean anything by it. I saw the recipe, and it struck a chord. Sorry for being a person."

"I don't know why you had to say anything at all," she mumbles, taking her copies and walking away.

Dinner that night doesn't come together the way I envision it, and I abandon the cooking plans halfway through. Ellen skipped lunch and is hungry, so we put on some reality show while waiting for the takeout delivery. She stops me after roughly thirty seconds of making out, which is never a good sign.

"Why are you doing that weird thing?"

"What weird thing?"

"I dunno. With your top lip, or something. Like an amphibian."

"What does that even mean, how would you know what an amphibian does?"

"Whatever. Just don't," she says. I nod, we resume, she stops again.

"I really don't know what you mean," I say, feeling around my mouth. "I mean, I did get a paper-cut today."

"I just wonder if maybe you should stop doing the copy machine gig," she says.

"Really? I don't think that's causing anything different."

"But aren't you sick of it? It seems monotonous."

"All jobs are monotonous."

She sighs, it's a big sigh. "I would just think you'd have other ambitions beyond this. They'll keep you doing this for a year, or forever, if you let them."

"It's not that bad of a gig, you know. I feel like I'm providing a useful and necessary service. Not many people can say that. I'm not expendable like they are. Plus, it's not making anything different. Not amphibious, certainly."

Her tone lightens at that, and we resume as normal, save for a firmness in her top lip I'd only been subconsciously aware of until now.

09

THE SOLITUDE OF FRUIT

Liz Kellebrew

THE SOLITUDE OF FRUIT

Liz Kellebrew

When the woman rolled over, something cold and hard pushed into her ribs. It was another body, bloated and stiff with rigor mortis. Every damn day she woke up with a new corpse in her bed and no idea how it got there. She'd given up on figuring out how they got in, and now she just worried about getting them out.

She drank her coffee in her long flannel nightgown with the mother-of-pearl buttons and the pink rosebud pattern, and she stared at the corpse. Its waxed handlebar mustache stuck out as rigidly as its other appendages. Yesterday's corpse had a Bob Marley tattoo on its shaved, bluish scalp.

It was getting harder and harder to dispose of these things. She could only put them in the dumpster every couple weeks or so, otherwise the cops started asking around. She'd stuffed most of them in her trunk and dumped them in the river, but she knew this was risky. In desperation, she'd also tried feeding parts of them to her cats, but only as a last resort.

As she wrangled the mustachioed corpse into a ninety-six-gallon garbage bag, its clothes and skin sloughed off in sticky pink piles on her white linoleum. She swallowed back bile and bent down to pick up the mess, but then she saw something extraordinary.

Instead of fat or muscle under its skin, the corpse was shiny and yellow. And it didn't smell like spoiled hamburger meat, but like sugar and starch. Its face peeled open like an overripe fruit, and where she expected to see a skull she saw a long, woody stem instead.

She hadn't seen such a brilliant yellow since her honeymoon in Puerto Rico, when she woke up early and watched the sunrise from the beach. The corpse no longer resembled a man so much as a massive banana just beginning to ripen, the smooth skin of its sides meeting in perfectly shaped ridges.

She hesitated a full minute before giving the corpse banana an experimental squeeze. But her touch left a deep brown bruise on its peel, and she drew back, chagrined. She wondered if it was squishy like a banana on the inside, too, but only seconds ago it had been a corpse. She should probably just throw it out.

When she tied the garbage bag over its stem, the banana let out a muffled scream.

She'd never heard a banana scream before. "Wha—what did you say?"

"I said, stand me up! I can't breathe!" it said in a high-pitched, helium voice.

Frantic, she helped the banana stand. It was wobbly at first, given the curvature of its body and its narrow base, but they figured it out. She untied the garbage bag and dropped it on the floor.

The banana was close to six foot three, not counting its stem. She knew this because, compared to her, the banana was the same height as her dead husband without his hat. She couldn't see its mouth, so she didn't know how it was speaking, but she could hear it just fine.

"You're not dead?" she asked, incredulous. Everyone she'd woken up to for the last six months had been dead.

"Of course I'm not dead," it squawked, indignant. "I'm right here, aren't I?"

She apologized and offered it a cup of coffee, which it absorbed through osmosis. When they finished their coffees and she took her emergency Valium, the banana insisted on going for a walk, but a couple test walks around the kitchen proved it couldn't get far on its own. The banana suffered a large bruise after falling into the refrigerator, so she made a square moving dolly from her roller skates and two serving spoons joined together with superglue and duct tape.

Even with its new wheels, the banana was quite naked, and the woman wasn't sure what would happen if the neighbors saw her pushing a giant nude banana down the sidewalk. So she dressed it in her husband's old trenchcoat, Panama hat, and gold-framed aviator sunglasses. After that, the banana didn't look much stranger than anyone else in New York.

The woman took the banana on a long walk. The sky was a brilliant blue and the breeze was just cold enough to make the woman wish for a scarf, but she didn't need one. She was no longer alone, and that was warmth enough.

In Central Park, they strolled under the orange brilliance of autumn leaves and watched ducks at the Reservoir. At the Met, they gazed at wall hangings made of macaw feathers from ancient Peru. They stopped for ice cream, and even though the woman felt awkward asking for a scoop of strawberry, it was okay because the banana ordered a banana split. When they arrived at Times Square, the banana confessed it was nervous around crowds, and the woman felt sorry because it was so easily bruised. They went back to her apartment and shared another pot of coffee.

In the weeks that followed, the woman began to question whether she'd done the right thing by dressing the banana in her husband's clothes. She knew she might be imagining things, but the banana was acting more and more like her dead husband every day.

For example, when the banana discovered the television, it spent its days chain-watching old episodes of *Law & Order* and *Survivor*. It demanded Pall Mall cigarettes, which the woman lit for it even though she couldn't figure out how the banana inhaled. The banana wanted meatloaf for dinner every night, drank a tumblerful of whisky before bed, and screeched at the cats whenever they got too close.

Even though the banana frightened the woman, the corpses stopped showing up when it slept next to her. She decided she could live with the banana's bizarre behavior.

One night, they went to bed after a special meatloaf the woman cooked with green peppers and onion. As she lay next to the banana, smelling its sweetness mixed with the scent of tobacco, she felt a wave of longing. It was quirky and odd, just like her own dear husband, and she thought she might be falling in love with the banana.

Had she really come to this? In love with a fruit?

But it wasn't like other bananas. It was tall, for one thing. And quite handsome when it cleaned up. It had good taste in movies and it could go on at great length about current affairs and the Yankees and the best steakhouses in Midtown, which gave it a competitive edge over most of the guys the woman had met in the pub across the street. Plus, the banana had chosen her, and that was something special in and of itself.

Overcome with equal parts fear and love, the woman reached out and rested her fingertips lightly on the banana's back peel.

Its stem stirred on the pillow. "What are you doing?"

The woman felt ready to explode, like a ripe plum in the sun. "I think I love you."

The banana said nothing. It rolled over slowly and looked at her with its eyeless, yellow face.

"I don't want to hurt you," she added quickly. The banana didn't want to get bruised. It might leave her.

"You can't hurt me. I'm a pretty tough guy," the banana said.

The woman couldn't tell if it was lying. She pulled back the sheet. "What about all these bruises?"

"What about 'em? That's life," the banana shrugged.

The woman's breathing came faster, and the blood pounded in her ears so loud she could barely think. She slipped her hand over its bare peel, her fingers tingling.

The banana flinched, but said nothing, so the woman kept going. She wrapped herself around its unprotesting body and it didn't stop her, even though she knew it must be in pain. She hugged it and wept and once she even called out her husband's name. That was her mistake. But the banana was gracious about it, ever the gentleman.

In the height of her passion, the woman tore off her flannel nightgown, but sadness rolled over her as she realized the banana couldn't take off its peel.

The banana sensed her frustration. "You can peel it. Just a little bit, at the side there."

The woman paused, feeling guilty. But the banana

laughed a squeaky laugh and sighed. "You know you want to," it said.

She did. She gently tugged at the peel where it bulged at its seam, and slipped her tongue in. He tasted even sweeter than she'd imagined, and she'd imagined the taste of bananas flambé in caramelized sugar with vanilla whipped cream on top.

The banana moaned, so she kept licking and nibbling until it screeched in ecstasy. Sated, the woman snuggled against the banana, and the two fell fast asleep just like they always did.

The next morning, the banana's peel was brown all over, and fruit flies gathered at the gash in its side.

The woman put on her nightgown and drank a strong cup of coffee. When she stopped crying, she laid the banana on the kitchen table, pulled off its peel, and scooped its flesh into three large mixing bowls. She made sixteen loaves of banana bread, which she had to bake one at a time because she only had one loaf pan.

Long after midnight, she put the last loaf in the oven. Then she folded the peel into a garbage bag and threw it in the dumpster.

RUBY GOES IN

Kate Gies

RUBY GOES IN

Kate Gies

Ruby likes to stick her finger in her belly button and swirl it around. She likes the feel of the rim and the steep fold inward. She likes the bitter lamb chop taste on her finger. Most of all, she likes to see how close she can get to the inside of herself.

Sometimes Ruby digs into the wormhole of her belly button with brisk finger thrusts until blood erupts like a tiny geyser. That's when she usually stops. But one day she keeps going and wiggles her finger down so far she hits something smooth and curved. A flush of excitement swims through her. She's in. She moves the tip of her finger lightly across the delicate surface. It's like soft boiled eggs, like rain-bloated worms, like jellyfish. When she tugs upward, her finger doesn't budge. Ruby thinks about what it would be like to live with a finger permanently in her belly button; she thinks it wouldn't be that bad. She presses in deeper and feels a sharp twang of nausea. Everything outside of her blurs, fades, muddles, and mutes. She throws up pebbly lumps. Ruby presses in deeper and fat phlegmy ropes envelop her finger. She twists the finger back and forth and the ropes slip and slither around it like hungry eels. Her body hums hot and bright and her ears fill up with the love songs of whales. Here she is. Just her. Inside the vastness of herself.

When her roommate comes home and sees her with her finger in her belly on the bloodied, barf-smeared couch, he turns grey, says *Jesusmotherfuckingmotherofgod,* and calls an ambulance to take her away.

In the ER, the doctor pushes down on Ruby's stomach and yanks her arm until her body releases her finger with the grunt of a fresh fart. She sits sullenly as the doctor sews stitches into her to gate her from herself. The doctor asks her what the hell she was thinking. He tells her that people he sees here have *real* problems. Stab wounds. Appendicitis. Heart attacks. They don't create problems for themselves. Ruby nods but she's barely listening. She's thinking about the oceans inside of her. How immense and wet and full she is beneath the surface.

GAZEBO

Shane Jones

GAZEBO

Shane Jones

I went on a ghost tour but no one else showed up. Huh, I said, to the guide, guess everyone else is a ghost. He didn't laugh because he was paid an extra dollar for every person who showed up. But he took me on the tour anyway. We walked through a wet cave and then through a rainy forest. I didn't see any ghosts. I know what you're thinking, said the guide, that this is a scam, but hey, look at that. He pointed and the sun appeared on his finger. Near a lake was a gazebo and stuffed inside the gazebo was my extended family. Levels of cousins clung to the roof, and babies I had never met crawled over each other on the floor between all the legs of more cousins, uncles, aunts, grandfather, and grandmother ghosts. Everyone is there but you, said the guide. My mother and father were so smashed together they looked like an uncle. My uncle tried to spin in place to make room for his stomach. But he couldn't move. A baby crawled up him and fell asleep on his stomach. Are they happy? I asked. Yeah, said the guide, they wouldn't show anything but happiness because they are incapable of anything else. Should I go in there? Up to you, said the guide, I'm not making anything extra now. The guide counted and then recounted his one dollar bill. I ran and dove into the gazebo. Everyone applauded but we didn't have cake. I felt lost even though I was touching everyone I came from. When I looked out of the gazebo, I saw another gazebo and in that gazebo was my three ex-wives, daughters, and son. There was so much room in that gazebo. Damn, said one of my cousins, you picked the wrong gazebo. Happens all the time, said my grandfather who turned from my grandmother and pointed to another gazebo with an entirely different family he had created. That's fucked, I said. Everyone in the gazebo started jumping to make me smile. They jumped together so high and so loud the gazebo jumped, and then hopped, across the field. Everyone held a baby and even some of the babies held babies. I just kind of stood there. On the way to the lake, I reached my hand out and grazed the faces of my ex-wives, daughters, and son. A line of silver glitter connected them.

THE MOTHER

Kathryn Hill

THE MOTHER

Kathryn Hill

I see you, short wide woman in the red day dress like you're a flagship or a thick red lip or a cello or a bird. I see that thin man, boyfriend, husband, click clicking pictures of you with your phone and those two curly-topped little girls, daughters, sisters, watching. I see you from the concrete bus stop bench across the street where I'm pinching at the swell of fat by the button on my jeans, staring at my sandwich from the Subway by CVS, wondering if I shouldn't just throw it away and starve whatever net of cells is multiplying under my belly.

I don't know what Dave is going to say. I don't know what he'll say when I tell him about going to the CVS and then going to Subway, ordering a six-inch turkey sub, asking for the bathroom key and then peeing into my drink cup, soaking the sponge-tipped test strip in my piss and waiting two minutes, looking-not-looking, seeing twin blue lines on the thin plastic screen, imagining the mess of cells between my hips in electric blues and yellows, hungry, voracious, with spiky skins and chromosomes like twisting eels, centers like the clear sludge of tomato hearts, dividing and dividing—and no, I don't know why I didn't call him right then, why I waited until I got home.

Or I could wait and never tell him. I could go to a clinic, get a pill, get scissors and a hose. I could beat my stomach against the backs of our kitchen chairs. I could wedge bunches of parsley up next to my cervix. I could suck down hundreds of vitamin C tablets. I could slide a penny up there. I could throw away my sandwich and starve it until its blues and yellows die.

But I know what Dave will say. He'll say it's a miracle our birth control failed, that our life will be so much better. He'll say he's been feeling like there's been something missing, like he hasn't been whole, or we've never really been whole, or both, and that he's always wanted to be a father, always dreamed of hearing me say those words, me showing him the double blue lines. And sure, we didn't think we'd be doing this right now, but he was ready, and he'd be okay if it were a boy or a girl, he didn't care, just as long as we could have one, have it together, that we could be a family because, you know, he barely had one.

But will he think this thing is a miracle when it finally becomes and comes out of me, when the thing rips my vagina like a broken zipper with its head, and I get lionfish stripes all over my sides, and my breasts shrink back once they run out of milk? Won't he be disgusted by my tits making milk? Will he be happy when he realizes he'll never see my collarbones or knuckles or knees ever again because pockets of fat made of cravings for pineapple and pickles and chilidogs will have consumed them? Doesn't he see that I'll be harder to love, that I'll be uglier to love, that I will constantly smell like vomit and shit? Won't he just go back to looking at skinny girl porn like he used to? Won't he just go back to looking at their thinness, their correct roundness, their drugged eyes and candied skin?

He'll start doing it next to me in bed, next to his fattened wife who smells like all the insides of his miracle child, stroking himself under the sheets that we share, knees up slightly to make the sheet taut, hiding himself, lying, telling me that he's not, that he hasn't, that he loves me, yes, he still does, don't I know that, how could I think otherwise? And I'll point out the tissue box he's been keeping next to our bed and the way he keeps his phone screen on low brightness and how he always seems to be clicking away to his desktop when I walk by. I'll say there's nothing in your search history. I'll say you sure look at your desktop a lot. I'll say you haven't touched me in weeks, and he'll say I thought you didn't want me to, I thought you were too upset, too busy with the baby and everything.

And I'll want him to touch me right then and leave me even sooner. I'll tell him to go, go away, because he'll put his hand on my shoulder, my stomach, my thigh, lightly, like I'm radioactive or glass, and I'll scream at him to go, run away to that ocean of pixels he can click through, zoom in on, watch fake-panting for hours, just pieces of bodies moving and wettening.

And I know he held my hands and promised he'd never look again, never look at those videos and cartoons and still shots with the trapped and skinny women. I know he said they didn't compare, that he saw them as something separate. But I remember what was on his screen when I first found him and cried. I remember the girl's deep collarbones, skinny, breakable, remember the pasties on her tits and the way her labia were lips, remember how her little skirt rode up, how the tops of her knee-highs didn't bulge with fat, how her giant tits bounced up and down in the man's liquid mouth, how her arms were tied away somewhere, skinny, breakable, her absent stomach, how much she was wanted.

And I know he's gone cold turkey, and he tells me that I am enough. But I also know a promise needs more than a kiss to last, and lying isn't that hard.

So I'm calculating the cost of finding him with his cock in his hand every day for the next forty years versus just going to a clinic next week, the cost of buying myself all new clothes, what I'd need for rent if he left me, or I left him, or both—when I see you across the street, short woman with the daughters, wide woman with the thin man, and I wonder if your life is beautiful like the pictures he's taking of you. I'm watching you let those little girls watch him take pictures where you are your whole body in the frames, where he obeys the rule of thirds, where he gets you with the sky, and you with that tall building, you with your rounded waist and the little bulge under your chin you got from eating macaroons and Thousand Island dressing when you were pregnant. I'm thinking your life is beautiful. I'm thinking he'll never leave you.

Before we married, Dave asked if I wanted to be a mother, have his children, have lots of children, four or five, adopt them if something went wrong, be foster parents even. He told me to imagine them with his curly hair and my smooth shoulders, imagine them calling me mommy, saying mama, saying first words with spaghetti sauce looped all over their faces. He said imagine them saying they love you.

And I lied. I told him I wanted them, wanted them badly, just like him. Said I'd always dreamed of being a mother, dreamed of being the one mine wasn't, everything she couldn't be, didn't want to be. I said I wanted a little girl, a little boy, two little girls, three little boys, four little five little six little people with barrettes and booboos and bugs who called me and cried for me and wanted me always because yeah, I'd barely had a family, either.

We kissed. We married. But I really just wanted—just want—Dave. Just us. Just him. Because what happens when I have this thing, this little Peter or Lilly or Sean or Charlotte, and I hate it, I really hate it, because it cries and shits and screams? Because every time we have sex I think of him fucking where its head came out? Because I think about my mother calling me fat girl, fat girl, fat girl? Because I think about being a liar, how I birthed an unloved child just to keep one lie instead of two?

But clinics are expensive and parsley's just a myth and he'd notice all the bruises if I forced the thing out with chairs or stairs or car doors. It would be easier to starve the thing to death slowly, inside me, in secret. Maybe start eating sandwiches without mayo, without cheese, without turkey or tomatoes or onions or peppers or bread—just eat the lettuce, slosh it around in my mouth and maybe swallow, maybe not. I could eat raw pasta like spears from the bag to stab the thing through and through. I could swallow a thousand black peppercorns so it itches and sneezes and dies. I could eat trays of ice cubes until it freezes to death in a fluid sac of red, solid ice.

Because Dave wouldn't love me anymore. Not if he knew I lied to him, not if I looked like a mother. I don't know how anyone could love a thing so much. I don't know how I could let myself be C-sectioned on a hospital bed, a slice through my belly, my intestines coming out first, my bladder, maybe my ovaries, sitting in bowls on a table next to me, my placenta wobbling on top of my belly before they close me back up. I don't know how one person could be worth so much. I wasn't worth so much to my mother. Neither was my sister. We were growths men had given her that had turned her into a cow.

That's what Joe called her. Joe called her cow and bitch and dirt. He was the last boyfriend my mother had when I was about seven and my sister was five. When he was around my mother would lock us in a downstairs room because sometimes he'd hit blood out of her. He'd leave and we'd unlock ourselves from the inside of wherever we were and fill a bowl with water, get the brown-red towel, go find our mother. Tina would just stand in the doorway and I'd soak the corners of the cloth, kneeling next to mother. Sometimes it was good to see her open in places, though, because it meant her body was full, that her body had blood, that it wasn't just hard bones and stretched skin and chipping fingernails.

Our mother had been fatless. She looked like all the slender bones and beams from model airplanes glued together with lips and hair. She cut Fig Newtons into thirds, ate orange Tic Tacs for lunch, a pint of blueberries in secret. She stretched herself at sharp angles in front of every mirror and street window, her eyes like periscopes, searching, scared.

She would watch me fiddle with my fatty belly skin, make me sit across from my sister at dinner to watch her munch Chips Ahoy and suck down plates of pasta, thin girl, while I split a piece of lettuce with my mother. She would break the thick white spine of the leaf with a butter knife, precise, exact halves, and we'd eat the lettuce together like a ceremony, like a prayer, watching my sister's lips gather crumbs and sauces and cheese, listening to the ocean of sloshing food as she chewed and chewed and swallowed. Sometimes my mother asked her to chew with her mouth open so she could watch, and my sister would do it and laugh, she would do it and cry afterwards.

My mother said that I was the baby who made her gain the weight. By the time I came out she said she was as big as a big boy tomato. But she said she didn't gain any weight right before or after Tina was born. Every time she said it, Tina would smile and hug herself tight, good daughter, skinny daughter. But our mother was so thin and sick when she was having Tina that my sister's teeth eventually came in without any enamel at all. And despite them being soft and small like white jellyfish in her mouth, our mother let Tina eat whatever she wanted because she was the thin girl who made her happy, the daughter who might have been loved.

Sometimes our mother would get sad, sadder than sad, thinner than thin, so I would hide tiny things in her collarbones when she fell asleep on the couch, little things like black raisins and yellow raisins and slimy red-eyed olives and Barbie shoes and buttons, little things like little weights to keep her home, keep her asleep, keep her away from windows and knives. Like the time I filled her collarbones with Coke and she woke up from the fizzing and popping and ice, or the time I filled her with all the wiry earrings and toe rings from her jewelry box, or the time she made a fat red lasagna with curly-edged noodles and oregano and beef for my sister but when she fell asleep my sister snuck a fork and we sisters ate almost half of it before she died on the couch. We didn't know she was dead for about a day. We called Aunt Jo the next night when the lasagna was gone and mom still hadn't gotten up. When Aunt Jo came over she said Oh God, Oh God. I had stuffed mom's collarbones with little

Legos and coins and Cheerios, stuffed her with Tic Tacs and blueberries and pieces of tape, and she looked like a sunk-skin dinosaur or a maze or a tide pool or a piece of chicken jerky. She looked swallowed, heavy, something eaten alive. Aunt Jo said Oh God, Oh God some more and held our mother's wrist and then cursed and then held a mirror under our mother's nose and nothing happened like it should have happened because our mother should have woken up because she was afraid of mirrors and cameras angled below her face.

When the ambulance people came and all the stuff fell off her shoulders and they said what is all this shit, my sister put her elbow over her eyes and pointed at me, but how could I explain hoping her collarbones sank to her stomach, hoping I could trap her like a firefly for a night if I just kept her weighted down in a jar?

So I'm sitting here waiting for the 55 bus, sandwich in my lap, striped pregnancy test in my purse, imagining this thing coming out of me someday with no teeth and no hair and no blood at all, a thousand tiny pieces of me and Dave swirling and becoming and dividing, heavy, when I see you across the street.

You, short wide woman in the red day dress. You and your soft upper arms and your bra that's too tight and your thighs that grow together under your dress. You don't put your hands on your hips to triangulate empty space at your waist. You don't hide the halo of your double chin when you smile. Your little girls are watching you. They are mesmerized. You are whole like milk. Your phone has jaguar print. You are beautiful, maybe. You are their mother.

I see you take the camera from the thin man and point your little girls to the curly-topped trees, not looking at those new pictures of you, not hunting them with eager, worried fingers. You hold the camera and start click clicking, the thin man laughing, his hand on your body of lobes and dimples and stretches and scars, your woman's body, happy, your fingers catching swirling little souls in the frames. You are a mother.

The next 55 bus going south gets here, and I sit in the row where the wheel wells breach so I can watch you and your family getting smaller.

I unwrap my sandwich. The mayo has made the bread soft like a belly, the bright yellow peppers sing acid into the air. I wonder if I should eat it. I imagine the electric cells inside me, small, smaller than small, their vacuoles and lysosomes and reticula eating, stretching, growing, stealing, becoming the stuff of knees and hands and lungs every minute, coming closer to a body, a boy or a girl, coming closer to making me a mother.

I wonder what kind of mother you are, short wide woman in the bright red dress, what you keep in your kitchen, what you cut-up crosswise for your daughters to eat with blunted pastel forks. I don't know what you'd tell a son, but I think you'd tell your daughters to eat. Tell them to eat until they can't see their bones, until their bodies are soft like baked pears with cinnamon and yogurt. Teach them to slurp balsamic vinaigrette out of salad bowls and scoop turkey gravy with their fingers. Tell them to eat everything. Say that everything is good for them. Give them Doritos and honey and beer and bananas foster and marble rye and Laffy Taffy and gum. Make sure they only drink whole milk, spread full-fat cream cheese on everything bagels. Tell them to fry everything in butter instead of olive oil. Show them how to be happy and big, big and happy, the fattest girls and the happiest girls, girls the size of stars. Their veins like udon noodles and their stomachs like cauliflower. Their fingers bunches of asparagus and their mouths French onion soup, teeth cheesy sourdough croutons, breath hot beef steam. They will have bay leaves in their hair and cardamom pods between their toes and meat lover's pizzas between their thighs. You will tell them they are beautiful and so they will be. You will tell them they are wanted, powerful, and so they will be. And you will be a mother who eats with them, who eats and eats and eats until you are their mother, as big as a house, a mother for your daughters to grow up in.

Maybe that thin man will leave you and go back to his pretty little ugly moaning things instead of eating at the table with you and your daughters—but that would be fine. You would be fine. You could live on the moon, live on food stamps. You could live and live and eat and eat and be their beautiful mother, their mother large like a sun birthing photons, like a wave that never crashes, like an indestructible refrigerator. Mothers are more like refrigerators than ovens or dogs or dirt.

I pinch my stomach and imagine all my undersides pumping and heating, churning and funneling, my body making a hungry past and future under my belly, a chaotic network of little things welling together, collecting, heavy, weighted down, little cells like little buttons and berries and electric faces holding everything I have been and Dave has been so closely together that our chromosomes twin and then split apart and apart and apart, run apart, explode apart making elbows and fists and hips and patellae, making something that will breathe, something that will maybe hate and maybe fear and maybe eat, maybe be beautiful, maybe be ugly, maybe be loved, maybe just be dead if I die, if I stop eating, if I die and am dead and am done, having died a truthful woman, a woman who did what was right, who did what she wanted, who never gave any man children, who never gained weight like mothers do or had blood hit out of her jaw or ear or nose or head like some children see their mothers hit or die empty like a cold hard stretch of moon on a couch, whose daughters didn't say anything for a long time after that, and didn't say much now with Tina in and out of rehab and everything, because they knew their mother died because she was their mother, because she couldn't starve them away, but she could starve herself. I could die, then, a mother who never brought a monster into the world. Or I could die later, a mother, full of sacrifice, empty of birth blood, with a rope or a gun or some pills, Dave happy with his little thing, me laughing somewhere up high in the stars, not fattening or thinning anymore, formless, thought about with wings and a halo, gold and silver and creamy white, remembered with love, remembered with anger, remembered with something like want.

I have two missed called on my phone from Dave. The bus goes over a bump and the sandwich jumps in my lap. I take a bite. I take a bite because I'm hungry. I take a bite because I am my mother, because I'm not you, not yet. The cold thin tomato eels its way between my teeth. I almost choke. I almost choke but I don't. I don't. I don't.

UNITED PARCEL SERVICE

Emily Koon

UNITED PARCEL SERVICE

Emily Koon

You aren't expecting the package, which looks heavy enough to contain a bomb or a brick of something. One of your *CSI* nightmares come to life.

"Maybe you ordered something off Amazon and forgot? Maybe someone's sent you a gift?" says the United Parcel Service driver, holding the box under his arm. Without asking, he steps into the foyer and sets the box on your Biedermeier hutch.

"Just need your John Hancock on this, and I'll be out of your hair," he says.

You've got death scenarios lined up for this. You're stabbed, excoriated, defenestrated. Twelve percent of murders are committed by strangers, according to that episode of *Dateline*. A woman selling a mattress through the classifieds was dismembered into 1-inch cubes and frozen in Zip-loc bags. For weeks, the police mistook her for salmon steaks. You write *Under Duress* on the tablet in case someone is tracking this.

No one's tracking this. A wire isn't tripped at UPS headquarters, signaling entry into a client's home. Quality Control or whoever handles breaches in protocol are at a teambuilding retreat when he lays the tablet on the box.

They're busy performing trust falls when he walks into your living room.

"Long day," he says. He collapses on the davenport and undoes the top button of his work shirt, exposing a wild triangle of chest hair. "Lady on Peach was returning some pants, and it was my fault they didn't fit, apparently. Now let's hear about *your* day." He pats the cushion beside him.

UPS drivers don't make themselves comfortable on people's davenports. People don't hear about it on the ten o'clock report and discuss it in checkout lines (*it was the damndest thing, how he took off his shoes and poured himself a gimlet*), yet on your davenport is a man in a brown shirt and shorts, singing a line from *La Boheme*.

"*O suoave fanciulla . . .*"

"Is there something else you need? A signature on an insurance form, maybe?" you ask. If he's thinking of torturing you, it's best to speak in pleasant tones.

"Can't think of anything," the driver says.

When the police arrive, he's sipping his gimlet and watching *Matlock*. The episode has Don Knotts in it, and there's been a mixup that Matlock will have to unravel.

"Ben Matlock, you sly devil," he says. He shakes his head at how easily Matlock gets the real killers, the grifters, the kidnappers to hang themselves. "I should have gone to law school. If I had, well, hindsight's twenty-twenty, am I right or am I right?"

The officer asks what the trouble seems to be. The driver looks up, annoyed that his program has been interrupted.

"We're having a disagreement about remodeling the kitchen, is what seems to be the trouble," he says. He takes a gulp of his gimlet as if to steady himself. "Marble countertops don't come cheap, I can tell you."

"That doesn't sound too serious," the officer says, his eyes searching your skin for signs of a fracas, his disapproval a fourth person in the room.

"But," you say.

"Sorry to have wasted your time, officer," the driver says.

As the police car backs out of the driveway, you think of the singles cruise you have coming up. You've paid for a month on the Aegean Sea, nothing but teal water fanning out like a skirt as far as the eye can see, everything your life contains disappearing beyond its edges. When you made the reservation, you sent energy into the universe about meeting a nice man. Someone tidy and liberal, who wouldn't put sweaty feet on your davenport. The person you had in mind was like Robert Downey, Jr. without the drug-laced past. Employed in the sciences, he was cerebral only to the point of being interesting, not making other people feel foolish. The set of fraternal twins you'd adopt together would be renamed Walter and Geraldine. You'll have to have a little talk with the universe.

. . .

You fantasize about a lot of awful things. In your scenarios you become the middle of the human centipede, an identify theft victim, the hostage in a bank robbery. Your car rolls into a lake while you're trapped inside. Your tether snaps during spacewalk at the International Space Station, sending you drifting into the cold vacuum of space. Sometimes on conference calls at work, you lose yourself in these catastrophes and have to be called back to reality.

"Sharon? Did we lose you? Where'd we land on the Winterson account?" says the Vice President of Development.

It happens on dates, too, the few you have a year.

"Sharon? Where'd we land on that second bottle of Zin?" say the brothers and college roomates of coworkers.

In each scenario, you plan an escape route. Convince the robber you're on his side, keep a hammer in the glove compartment. Pass on the second bottle of Zin. The only scenario you don't plan for is a delivery person delivering himself, making you sign for him. Putting sweaty feet all over your davenport.

.   .   .

Your house is a fortress the driver picks his way into each night. He tries his key and finds you've had the locks changed again. You've installed an alarm system, requiring him to cut power to the house. When he finally gets inside, he pours a gimlet and flops on the davenport, where he lets out a satisfied sigh. "The people rest, your honor." Something he lifted from *Matlock.*

You try putting the house on the market. A nice thirtysomething couple called Knickerbocker comes to see it, their hope for the future beading on their skin like sweat. They're looking for a place with "good energy." You worry they'll see the driver sprawled on the davenport in the bottom half of his uniform and assume he comes with the house.

When the real estate agent brings the Knickerbockers inside, the driver tells them there's been some kind of mix-up.

"We love this house. We'd never sell it," he says.

The Knickerbockers fold themselves back into the agent's Miata and buy the Tudor revival on the corner.

Eventually, you accept that you live together. At 5:20 each afternoon, the brown truck rolls into the yard, and he removes his shoes and socks. Gimlet, davenport, *Matlock*. During the first year you think about purchasing a gun to scare him off but decide against it. If things turned ugly, you'd go up for Murder One.

"There isn't much you can do now. He's got squatter's rights," your lawyer says, after the driver has been in your house five years. There will be other lawyers, and they'll all say the same thing.

.   .   .

On your thirtieth anniversary, the driver gives you a pearl necklace. Not to garotte you with, it turns out, but a gift of love. You're only common law, but to him this is as real as if you had a church wedding with tulle rice bundles and a woman named Beverly warbling *The Lord's Prayer*.

The driver is old and tired from carrying around an enlarged prostate. On the left side of his body, ulcerous tumors eat into his arm and face. The doctor has scraped them off, but all those years driving in the sun have destroyed the skin at its deepest layers. The tumors always come back, whatever he does to get rid of them.

His muscles hang flaccid from his bones. You could tear him like tissue paper. Just yesterday he slipped a disc trying to move the davenport. To get the job done, you had to enlist the Knickerbocker man. Now you think you could have moved the davenport yourself. You feel strong enough to throw a Biedermeier hutch.

You throw the pearls instead. Into the fire, built by

the driver's own hoping-for-romance hands. Why did he think he'd get some? In all these years, you've never let him touch you.

The pearls blacken in the fire, holding together until the string burns away and the tiny black globes bounce off the hearth. You once read that breaking a string of pearls was a bad omen, a sign everything is about to fall apart. You don't know what it means to burn one, if that makes things worse, and if it does, for who?

"Sharon, that's a genuine Mikimoto! Have you lost your marbles?" the driver says.

He picks up the hot black pearls and cleans the soot off them with spit, protecting them in his cupped palm. Pearls don't burn, was the other thing you read. It's how you know they're genuine.

"It's nice, but I'd rather you moved out," you say.

The driver looks up, a thumb-shaped smudge of soot under his lip. His mouth hangs open, weighted down by jowls. "I'm eighty years old. Where would I go?"

"The old folks' home? The YMCA? A halfway house?"

When he tries to get back on the davenport, you kick him in the shin.

"You're cracked, Sharon. *Non compos mentis.* What's gotten into you?" he says, rubbing the kick mark on his lower leg.

"Stay off my davenport." You kick the other shin.

The driver ends up on the floor, cradling his shins. A line appears on the carpet in front of you, with everything that's already happened in your life on one side and everything that's yet to be on the other. You know your next move will define you as a person, one who allows herself to be carried by the current of time or who pilots her own existence. Taking the road less traveled, like in the poem.

You want to kick the driver's scrotum, but there isn't time for that. You open the door and roll him outside in the carpet. When he's climbed back up the hill and sees you've barred the door with the davenport, he gets into the UPS truck, by now an old junker. The engine turns over after the fifth or sixth crank, and then he's gone.

■　■　■

When word gets around you've kicked the driver out, the picketers come.

"The old folks' home was full, you jerk," they say. He's been living in the truck next to the Wal-Mart, and they've set up a crowdfunding campaign to get him back on his feet.

"You're a monster," they shout.

"He let himself in. I couldn't get him to leave," you insist.

"You're full of it."

They demand to see the bruises, the shiners, the locksmith receipts. How can they take your word for anything they can't see with their own eyes? You try turning the question around on them—how can you trust they're who they say they are, not monsters themselves— but they turn it back around, how you don't get to ask them things, how you don't have the right.

"Come out, lady," they shout. "These signs took us hours to make."

What a disappointment you must be, sealing yourself up inside the house, your experience taping curtains around windows finally good for something. The picketers give up and start circling a vacant lot. When the lot is filled with modular housing, they move on the quarry, which they claim is a safety hazard. No one has fallen in since that one kid ten years back, who rolled down the side like a big log and into a pile of department store mannequins. If you're remembering the story correctly, he climbed out on his own, more embarrassed than hurt.

"That doesn't make it ok to leave a giant hole in the earth," the picketers insist. "One tragic accident would be one too many."

The hole is filled in with earth and turned into a skating rink, and so on and so on, until the world is exactly how they want it.

■　■　■

One day you're sweeping the foyer and notice the package still sitting on the hutch, a coating of dust on the outside and the corners mouse-chewed. You're expecting a cloud of anthrax or a poison dart flicked from a miniature catapult but find only a bathing suit with a parrot embroidered on the front, a floppy coral sunhat and espadrilles.

"The trip!"

The singles cruise, how could you have forgotten? It was to Greece, you think. No, Cyprus. Or was it Italy? Something about teal water fanning out around you. A water skirt. You planned to tell people you met on the boat your name was Vivian. Women named Vivian were always sure of themselves, grabbing life by the balls, so to speak, and you liked the idea of pretending to be someone like that. You thought if enough people called you Vivian that's who you'd eventually become.

You slip out of your housecoat and into the bathing suit. It doesn't fit, but that's not the point.

. . .

You've been a shut-in so long many of the neighbors don't know who you are. If they do, they know only of a scandal years back, a black widow who hid inside until she became a brown recluse. You aren't sure what stories have sprouted from you and walked away on vines, how near or far from the truth they've flowered, but they aren't good stories, you know that.

"Ma'am, do you need help? Do you need something?" the neighbors ask as you walk toward the highway in the parrot bathing suit and the espadrilles and the floppy hat.

"Not a thing," you say. You walk in the direction you think blue water might be.

When you've left the town behind, you're in a wilderness in which you're not afraid because bear attacks are at a century low. Sex slavers are unlikely to be interested in you.

"Who'd abduct an old woman?" you ask the trees, who don't answer. They've got their own problems. They're disappearing row by row, recycled into condominiums with ocean views.

You wonder what far-off place you're pointed at. The Black Sea, perhaps? You've always wanted to see if for yourself, to find out if the water is really black or that's just what people call it. In your mind it's a glittering purple-black ocean filled with scorched pearls.

You press on into the forest. Every now and then a hiker or government surveyor comes along and asks if you're all right. Have you wandered off from your caregivers? Lost your dementia pills in the woods? Can they give you a ride to the old folks' home?

"No, not there," you say, putting as much space between you and them as you can. "The driver might be living there."

After the quarry, the picketers had picketed the old folks' home and shamed the owners into building an addition. You worry the driver would move into your room and everything would start all over again.

You keep walking until the woods peter into an apricot beach rimming an ocean. You blink in the bright sunlight, all those years as a shut-in having accustomed you to dimness. The water shifts from blue to ultramarine to bright moss green at its edges, and on the opposite shore sprout the cobalt blue domes of houses. There are people at the water's edge waving you to them, chanting something that sounds like *Vi-vi-an, Vi-vi-an, Vi-vi-an*.

It's easy as pie, sliding into the warm water. Looking back, you see the apricot beach expanding, engulfing the forest and the town with the old folks' home, the driver and your davenport and the Knickerbockers, until everything your life once contained is buried. The sand takes the picketers and the old quarry, the house you grew up in on Plum Street with the red gingham curtains in the kitchen window, the nieces and nephews in distant cities. It blankets the high school where you once played a solo on the French horn and the office building you worked in until you retired, with its labyrinth of gray cubicles folding back on itself. All these pieces of your life sink beneath the sand, slipping out of your head as you circle your arms in the deepening water and push toward the other shore.

TINY LITTLE GOAT

Jasmine Sawers

TINY LITTLE GOAT

Jasmine Sawers

After you left, a goat took up residence in the left ventricle of my heart.

I didn't know about my little stowaway at first. I thought I simply wished to say "no" more often and while screaming. I thought the quality of my enunciation had merely slipped the same way my housekeeping had. I thought I was finally becoming the curmudgeonly old man I had dreamt of being since I was a little girl. Freedom, I thought, is no pants and a tin can to chew on.

I lost feeling in my extremities. Brown fingertips and little mushroom toes went pale purple, lavender maybe—quite nice a color if I were a flower, which I'm not. On a good day, I am a person.

"We care about you," some of my friends said.

"We know this is hard," said others.

"You need to get this shit looked at it," said the best ones. "It ain't right." That's how I ended up on my back in an MRI machine, which is a tube that contains more than its fair share of dread.

"Aw," the doctor said. "There he is."

"What?" I said. "Abort it!"

"It's not a baby," said a friend. "Oh my God. Look at

it. It's so cute."

"It's a tiny little goat," said the doctor. "Right in your heart. That's the *organ* that pumps *blood* through your *body*."

"I know what a heart is," I said. "Why is there a goat in it?"

"Same as any parasite," the doctor said. "Not exactly run of the mill, but this sort of thing is not actually that uncommon. A simple surgical procedure and you'll be good as new."

I was rolled out of the MRI machine and shown a picture of my goat. He'd taken a great big shit right in my inferior vena cava. He was chewing on some grass. He was wall-eyed and smiling.

"What happens when you take him out?" I asked.

"You get a sticker and go home," said the doctor. "That's where you *live*."

"No, I mean what happens to him? Do you give him to a petting zoo or something?"

"Oh my, no," said the doctor. "He'll die instantly. That means *right away*."

"What happens if I don't get rid of him, then?"

"You'll die gradually," the doctor said.

"That means *real slow*," my friend said.

"You'll stop being able to see colors," the doctor said. "Food won't taste like anything. You'll be tired all the time on account of his blocking up your blood flow. And in the end, you'll just fade away."

"And the goat?"

"He'll burst out of your ribcage and terrorize the town in a fit of bloodlust."

"Just schedule the surgery," my friend said. "Everything will look better without a goat in your heart."

But I went home that night and I took a piss on my grandma's antique davenport. I took off all my clothes and wandered out into the yard. I left the door open. I followed the scent of sweet clover.

ONCE UPON A TIME IN AN ORCHARD

Jasmine Sawers

ONCE UPON A TIME IN AN ORCHARD

Jasmine Sawers

Every apple is poisoned here.

That's misleading. I mean to say, every apple in my orchard comes pre-poisoned for your convenience. A simple genetic modification and these beauties burst from the branch as shining and deadly as the grin of a woman. Note their size: no monstrous supermarket apples here. These fit just so into the palm of any delicate princess on the run. But don't let that fool you—there are no apples richer, or fuller, or more fragrant. Here, breathe deeply.

This is the smell of summer when she was a child. This is catching fireflies in jars at twilight and lighting the path through the garden with them. This is getting lost in the honeysuckle and lilac and finding her way home by the spill of hydrangea. This is tiptoeing barefoot outside at first light and feeling the dew cool between her toes. This is juice running down her chin.

She'll close her eyes. She'll set red lips to firm flesh and hold the scent of it in her lungs for the length of three heartbeats. Before she breaks the skin with her teeth, she'll thank you.

RAIN CLOUD

Ingrid Jendrzejewski

RAIN CLOUD

Ingrid Jendrzejewski

Yesterday, I became a rain cloud. I hadn't realized that it was a democratically elected position, but then there are a lot of things I don't know about nature. The sun put me forward, and the horizon seconded the nomination. I had a bit of trouble winning over the mountains and prairies due to my lack of experience, but the votes swept in from the stars and forests and tides, and in the end, I came out ahead, by a decided margin. So I quit my job, informed my family, then took off my clothes and ascended to the heavens.

It's cold up here, but the winds say I'll get used to it. I've managed to look reasonably gray and foreboding and have floated menacingly over pedestrians and picnics. However, I have yet to figure out how to rain. There's something about it that seems so impossible, so unlike anything I've ever done. But the universe seems to have confidence in me. It will come in time, says the sun. Just let yourself go, say the stars. After all, says the horizon, humans are made of water and there is sadness ahead. Raining isn't so different than crying; you just do it with your whole body.

HER
BLOOD

Maryse Meijer

HER BLOOD

Maryse Meijer

Excuse me? she said. Help, I need—can you help me?

She was standing at the side of the counter, in the hallway that led to the booths and the bathroom. A very small woman, a girl, I thought, at first, with this thin dishwater hair hanging to her waist. Blood pasting her white jeans to her thighs. She was hunched almost double, her arms wrapped around her waist, and through that limp hair lashing her face she smiled around a crop of bucked teeth. A drop of saliva looped to the floor and she put her wrist to her mouth. Sorry, she said, sucking spit off her lip. I'm sorry.

Did you call someone? I asked. Her hands, veined like a man's and black beneath the nails, crept to her pockets.

I don't know, she said, I think I dropped it, in there— and she nodded toward the hall where the bathroom was, the black door hanging open. I leaned over the side of the counter and looked, not because I wanted to see what was in that room, but because I wanted to not see her for a moment, those dark stains all the way to her ankles, that mouth with its wild grin. The smell of burning sausage from the ovens made me gag. I could see nothing through the door and I looked back at her and saw her socks, by accident, how they were growing red all over the white.

I didn't know what it meant. I kept thinking she'd cut herself or fallen on something.

I had a miscarriage, she said. In your bathroom?

I imagined a full-grown baby in there, slick and cracked on the black tile. In some way I didn't really understand what a miscarriage was. How it was different than giving birth. Her stomach was curved inward, away from her crossed arms, like an animal that didn't want to be touched. I was stuck, staring at her, my body more cement than flesh.

Maybe you could call someone? she suggested, polite, her voice very small, high, like a child's. An ambulance?

Okay, I said, reaching for the wall phone, okay—

I turned the OPEN sign off and sat with her in a booth. All I could think of was how the seat would take the stuff coming out of her, how the splits in the vinyl would soak up her blood right down into the foam and what could I do about that, really, I would have to tell Jason and he would be pissed, like I'd spilled my own blood there on purpose. I didn't think to put down a towel or give her a glass of water or ask her how she was feeling. I wasn't thinking anything. The girl trembled next to me with her knees tight together, making a sound like *hm, hm*, over and over, not the sound of something in pain but something purely surprised. Hm, she said, her elbows tucked tight against her sides and her hands clasped at her knees, her red thighs the same size as her calves. She bent over the tabletop to look out the window, neon from the shop signs opposite us pooling in the wet gutters.

Do you think they're coming? she asked, and then put her hands to her forehead for a minute as she took a deep breath. I saw that even her hair was red in places, where she'd sat on it, or where she'd brushed it back with her hands. I moved away a little, to the very edge of the seat, and she said I'm sorry, I'm so sorry, and I had to go on sitting there, wondering if the blood coming from her was going to touch my own jeans.

When the ambulance stopped at the curb I could see two men through the window, heads down in the rain, hurrying to the door in their blue suits. One of them was laughing at something the other said. Oh, she said, sitting up straight, and the men were in the room, dripping onto the mats, and I got out of the booth so they could get to her, the men were touching her arms and asking her questions, and she was nodding and whispering; her eyes slid over to me and she tried to smile.

I spent an hour on my knees in the bathroom, with a bucket of bleach and paper towels and a pair of old yellow gloves with crud in the fingertips. I wiped the porcelain over and over with one hand while I breathed into my elbow. There was something the size of steak in the toilet, sunk in the red water, more like an organ than a baby, and then I realized, no, of course it wasn't a baby, but maybe there was something like a baby inside, something the size of a quarter, a dot of an eye, a tail. I coughed and flushed. The thing squeezed down the pipe, and little bits of whatever it was gurgled back up into the pit of the bowl so that I had to stand there and flush again and again until the water was clear.

I looked around. She'd used all the toilet paper, stuffed long red ropes of it into the trash. There were meat-colored streaks all over the floor. And all the graffiti on the walls that Jason loved—we never cleaned it off or re-pained— that is what she had to look at while it happened, things like *You're a shit* and *All you cunts!!* in big gold script. The dark red walls were almost black in the windowless room, and I knew I wasn't seeing it all, getting it all, the mess she'd made, but I couldn't be in there any more, so I left. I took the trash out to the dumpsters and ate cold pepperoni and drank a cup of Mountain Dew standing up at the counter. The phone rang.

Hi, she said, and I spit the pepperoni into a napkin. Her voice was excited, whispery but loud, like she had her mouth right up against the receiver. Hi, it's you?

Yes, I said, how—

I'm fine, she said, breathless. I'm sorry, she said, I know—there was a mess. I would have cleaned it. I would have—

It's fine, I interrupted. Are you okay?

Oh yes, she said. Yes. I'll be just perfect, she said.

That's good, I mumbled.

Thank you for helping me.

It's fine, I said again, and she stayed on the line for a moment, and so did I, listening to her, listening to her listening to me, and then she made a noise, like a part of a laugh, or a sigh, some swallowed sound, and then she hung up.

I walked home with the hood of my sweater up, slowly getting soaked, the toes of my sneakers turning black in the filthy puddles. Everything was closed and there seemed be no one anywhere on the street. Now that I worked night shift, I was always alone. I imagined having what she had, a place in my body that shook out blood and tissue, that could splash an entire room with my insides and then let me walk away. I tried to think about how it would feel, waiting for that part of me to be done with itself. I got an erection though I didn't mean to. I pushed my hands into the front pocket of my hoodie and rubbed them against my crotch, stretching the sweater down, grimacing, not feeling good, not feeling good at all, and then I left it; I got to my apartment and fell on the couch in my wet clothes and went to sleep.

The next time I saw her she wasn't alone. Her boyfriend or husband was a giant next to her, well over six feet, with a thick red beard and red hair curling down over his ears and a gut of hard fat stacked over the belt of his khakis. She was pressed up to his side, in a tank top and a short corduroy skirt, showing off her flat chest and pale legs. She looked a little older in the daytime, I thought, maybe mid-twenties. She came up to the guy's armpit. He ordered a slice of the Five Meat and she wanted a diet Coke. He took their change and I gave her a cup and her skin touched mine, dry thin skin, and she smiled through her hair at me. She never really stopped looking at me, even when they sat down in a booth, and he started eating and talking through a mouth full of food about some band they were going to see. I turned away to get some pizzas from the freezer, but I could feel her gaze crawling up my neck. I was angry but didn't know why; maybe it just felt like they were showing off, coming back here. Either he didn't know what had happened or he didn't care. She made sure I'd see her but couldn't talk to her. I thought maybe she was really crazy. I heard the noise from the street rush through the opening door, and I looked up finally, and her head was turned over her shoulder, hair grazing her ass. I looked for the blood but of course it wasn't there, and she was still smiling at me, and I smiled, out of habit, back.

They came in almost every day. He got the same slice, and she never ate anything, just spun her cup of Diet Coke between her hands, crunching her ice. There was tape now over the split in the foam seat she had sat on and that was the booth they always took, I'd wiped down that night, her blood scaled on the vinyl and then clinging to the rag. They both seemed amped up, giddy; they talked and laughed and used their hands a lot and were never quiet, never still. Maybe they took drugs. She was always falling into him, stumbling against his back, like she was desperate to get her body on his. And he was always grabbing her bony wrists, to pull across the table for a kiss, to steer her where he wanted her to go, her body jerking in response to his like a puppet. The counter came all the way up to her chest, and when they ordered she stood there kneading the edge of the counter with her thumbs in this slow weird way. Like that first night, I didn't know what to do. I served her, I served her boyfriend. I cleaned up after them—their dirty plates, their crushed napkins—I let them smear themselves all over the place. She had a habit of putting her forehead right on the glass window when she looked out of it. The grease from her face left a mark and I wiped that off, too.

I didn't see them kissing or holding hands. There was something sexless about them individually, maybe just because I thought they were unattractive, him especially, with his outsized body and ugly clothes and filthy beard, but at the same time I knew they were fucking a lot. He was constantly grinning at her like he was thinking about something dirty they had just done together. Her hair climbed all over his suede coat. If he was on top of her—I tried to imagine it. I imagined it against my will. How could it not hurt her? I was nineteen. I didn't know what it was like. I kept walking home in a daze, tripping over the holes in the street, thinking about being crouched next to the toilet and scrubbing all that stuff off it, all that stuff that came from her. I tried to remember when she had walked in, if she had ordered anything, if I had seen her—I must have seen her, it's a small shop, and almost always empty—but there was nothing, just the image of her on the first night after it happened, when she was just leftovers of a person, as if she had come undone there in the bathroom and had to gather herself, piece by piece, back together, stuffed into her jeans, minus what she left in the toilet, what she left for me.

I wasn't cleaning the bathroom or going in there at all. I peed into a Styrofoam cup on my breaks. During the shift overlap I watched the others tick off their names on the bathroom maintenance clipboard but I didn't tick mine. Someone must have called Jason, who'd been out of town when all this stuff happened, and he came in at the end of my shift and started saying he couldn't trust me if I started slacking off whenever he went out of town. I stood against the wall and nodded. Jason went to take a piss. I heard the door open, and I stood very still at the counter. I heard his boots circling. What the fuck, he said, and the door banged against the wall as he came back out. The toilet's fucking clogged, he said. I didn't move. He snapped his fingers. Hey. Genius. Wake up. He kicked the plunger into the hallway and I said I'd take care of it. I don't remember if I did. I don't remember ever going back in there again.

But she did. Both of them did. Once they went in there together, and I could hear him laugh, and when they came out she was licking her lips and giggling. Though when she saw me looking she stopped, like she'd been caught. A muscle in her cheek ticked and her lips were struggling to get around her bucked teeth. I kept staring at her. He was leaning over the stack of flyers on the deep windowsill, one of his feet in the air, and he was trying to get her to laugh about something he saw there, and she was caught between the two of us, between me and him, me and the black door behind her.

She called me again. She knew that I was alone or didn't care that I wasn't. If someone else had picked up, would she talk to him instead? How did she really know my voice? We'd hardly ever talked to each other. And yet we both knew.

You're there, good, you're there, she said, and it was like the time she called from the hospital or wherever; she was a little out of breath, her mouth right up to the phone. The way her teeth were, she couldn't quite get her lips over them, and so there was always this sound, of her trying to pull her mouth around those teeth, a very wet sloppy sound. I listened.

It's late, she said, I can't believe you work so late.

You're up.

Oh, well, I don't like to go to bed, I'm always up, she said, and giggled.

What about your boyfriend?

My boyfriend?

The guy you're with.

You mean Dennis, that's Dennis. Her *s*'s hissed a little, almost a lisp. He's not here.

Does he know?

About—?

About when you were here before.

Oh, she said, no. I mean not really.

I didn't ask what that meant. *Not really.*

I used to come in before, she said, tentative, almost a question. By myself?

You did?

Don't you remember?

A lot?

A few—I work near you. I mean I saw you so many times.

I was sure I would have recognized her. Someone that looked like her. I had a feeling she was lying but I couldn't say that so I didn't say anything, just dug my finger beneath a broken flap of plastic on the register drawer.

He didn't know that, she said. He thought it was his idea. To go there. He likes your pizza.

It's not my pizza. It comes frozen.

Well, he likes it. Do you mind? I mean, that we come in so much? That I'm calling? You must be busy, she said. You're always by yourself. It's a lot of work, she continued, firmly, as if telling me something I didn't know.

It's fine, I said. You work down here, too? Where?

She paused. Just down the street, she answered. Not far at all.

Where do you live?

Not far, she repeated.

I broke open a sleeve of Styrofoam cups with one hand. Why are you calling? I mean do you want something?

No, she said. I just thought—

Nevermind, it's fine, I said, stacking the cups next to the register. I thought about the way she'd sat in the booth, holding her knees so tight together, the metal smell of her so strong I had to breathe through my mouth. I pushed the cups into line with my finger. There was a dustless circle where they always stood and I had to get them into that circle. We didn't have lids or straws. Jason thought they were a waste of money. Every day I cleaned up spilled soda from the table and booths and floor. The rain was sliding down the front window in thick ropes, and I flexed my toes in my shoes, still wet from the night before. It would not stop raining.

I started imagining that this was some kind of game for them, that he would fuck her and she'd get pregnant and she'd take something, medicine or something, and they'd wait for the thing to happen. He'd send her into these places to do it in public, pour the thing out of her, and he'd meet her at the hospital, and she'd tell him who had touched her and what it felt like, and he'd fuck her again right away, as soon as they got home, and there'd be a pile somewhere, of her jeans, stiff, rust-colored, that she would never wash or throw away. They were crazy, dirty, the smell of stale blood in their bedroom and the fact of her pain just that, a fact, and not something that could really hurt her, because she'd been scraped out so often that everything breakable had already been broken and cleared away. She would be smooth inside, as smooth and slick as wet rock. Which was a weird thing to think but there was something, something fucked up about them, about her, the way she smiled at me with her boyfriend standing right there, as if we'd met at a party, as if we were friends, as if what had happened had never really happened at all.

I didn't have an umbrella, and I never got one. Jason said it was monsoon season, and I thought that was a real thing until I looked it up online and saw that it was only for India. I used that joke with her the next time they came in. Dennis leaned against the counter and said Goddamn rain, right man? And I said yeah, it's like a fucking monsoon out there, and she seemed pleased, laughing with her mouth wide open. I slung his pizza onto a paper plate and didn't charge her for her soda. He clapped my shoulder and said You're a good guy. She put her arms around his bicep and beamed. I was almost in a good mood. They'd tracked in a lot of mud, and while they ate I got the mop and cleaned the floor, swabbing beneath their table so they had to raise their feet, before settling them back onto the wet tile, making new marks.

Do you have friends? she asked me that night, on the phone. A lot of friends?

I tucked the phone against my shoulder, counting money from the drawer. I have roommates, I said. Two.

Boys?

Yeah.

Are they home when you get home?

What?

She smiles. I'm sorry, she says, I just—thought of you as going home by yourself.

They go out a lot. It's mostly just me.

I never lived with other girls. I went from home to being with Dennis.

Are you married?

In a way, she said. I put the money in the bank bag, zipped it, tucked it into the safe. The phone hurt my shoulder when I held it that way, without hands, and because I was sweating my ear stuck to the receiver.

We met at a concert, she told me. I was dancing and someone hit me on my cheek, with her bracelet or her ring or something, and I had a cut and Dennis helped me fix it up. I could hear her smiling. I could imagine her holding her hand to her face, lost in a crowd, people slamming around her, into her. I imagined being there, drinking a beer, watching her from a spot against the wall. I'd see her get hit and I wouldn't help her. I would just watch the wound open up in her face, and I'd want to keep watching, but Dennis would come in between us, to clean her up. It's not that I liked or wanted to see her get hurt. There was just something about it that got to me. I couldn't get away from it. The sound she made, the smallness, all that mess, her huge eyes in that horsey face filled with a remote terror as the ambulance men took her away and she just smiled and smiled.

Was it your first time?

My first time what?

Having, you know—it happen.

I could hear her shifting, her clothes rubbing against a chair or a couch. I wondered if her hair was in her face, like it always was when I saw her, or if it was pulled back, and, if so, what her face was like when it was bare, if there was something behind all that hair that she was hiding.

I didn't even know that I was pregnant. I thought I was dying, she said, and laughed softly. I really did. I was never regular, in that way, you know, I didn't keep track because—it didn't matter. I'm just really sorry, I did try to clean up, but more was—was coming, and I didn't know if it would stop. And it was so dark in there. And I wasn't thinking right.

Are you really, though? Sorry?

Hm?

I mean, you keep saying it. I just wondered if that was true, I said. It's like you're happy it happened, like you— like you liked it.

She took a breath and held it. I winced into her silence. When had I ever talked back to a girl? A woman? When I had ever said what I wanted to say, even if I didn't mean it?

I should go, she said, her voice moving away—she was already dropping the phone as she spoke, I could hear it hit the floor, and she didn't hang up, I had to do it, though—I listened for a long time, imagining her face down on a bed, her torso twisted into the blanket, seething into her pillow.

But she called back, an hour later. When the phone rang I didn't say Hello Party Pizza like I usually did. I just waited.

I think I know what you meant, she said, reasonably, as if we hadn't been interrupted. You think I'd just leave you alone. You think I'd—do something different. Not be able to go back there. She paused. But I do. I can't help it. I love it, she said in that breathless whisper, and I was suddenly so hard it hurt.

Why?

I don't know! she exclaimed in wonder. The way you look at me. Do you know how you do it? Is it something you do on purpose?

What?

Like—like you hate me, she said, swallowing a last giggle. Like you can't stop.

I don't hate you.

Oh, it doesn't matter. Maybe there's a different word for it. For that way you look.

I wiped the counter with a paper towel, in a circle, the same circle over and over.

Did you look?

At what?

When you were cleaning up, she said. Did you see anything?

I thought of the black shape in the water, its gleaming sides. Not really, I said.

I did, she said, sniffing, matter-of-fact, something wet-sounding at the back of her throat. I touched it, even. I thought it would be, you know, that you could see what it looked like. But it wasn't a fetus. It was something else. No one had ever really told me—her voice broke off, and there was a scratching sound, like her nails against a piece of paper.

But it's—normal?

Yes, she said. I guess so. It would have been so small, you know, the actual—thing. It must have been inside there somewhere. And you—she swallowed. You just—flushed it, right?

Yeah, I—I mean, you left it there, I—

She laughed. No, I mean, of course, right. Right.

Did it hurt a lot?

Yes, she said. Do you want children? she whispered.

No, I said.

You're lucky, she said, thoughtful, her voice dropping down more, thinning out, a wisp, floating away from me.

I love you, I said, squeezing my eyes shut, and she exhaled, not surprised, not unhappy, and for a moment I thought I had a chance, the future bloomed out before me, and then she said He's home, and hung up.

[contributor bios]

Samantha Duncan's latest poetry chapbook is *The Birth Creatures* (Agape Editions, 2016), and her fiction has appeared in *Meridian*, *The Pinch*, and *Flapperhouse*. She serves as Executive Editor for ELJ Publications and reads for *Gigantic Sequins*, and she lives in Houston.

Kate Gies lives in Toronto, where she writes and teaches creative non-fiction at George Brown College. Her work has most recently appeared in *Word Riot* and *Ascent Aspirations Magazine*.

Kathryn Hill is an MFA candidate in fiction at Arizona State University where she also reads prose for *Hayden's Ferry Review*. Her flash fiction has appeared or is forthcoming at *AGNI Online*, *Gigantic Sequins*, *Monkeybicycle*, *Passages North*, and elsewhere. She has creative nonfiction forthcoming in an anthology from *Outpost19*. Follow her on Twitter at @kathelizhill

Ingrid Jendrzejewski likes cryptic crosswords, the game of go and the python programming language, among other things. Links to her work can be found at www.ingridj.com and she occasionally tweets from @ LunchOnTuesday. Recently, she was awarded the A Room of Her Own Foundation's Orlando Prize for Flash Fiction and the Bath Flash Fiction Award.

[contributor bios]

Shane Jones is the author of the novels *Light Boxes* (Penguin, 2010), *Daniel Fights a Hurricane* (Penguin, 2012), and *Crystal Eaters* (Two Dollar Radio, 2014). Fiction and non-fiction has been published by *VICE, The Paris Review Daily, Washington Square Review, LIT, The Portland Review, The Believer Logger, Quarterly West*, and *DIAGRAM*. He lives in upstate New York.

Liz Kellebrew holds an MFA in Creative Writing from Goddard College. She lives in Seattle and writes fiction, poetry, literary essays, and creative nonfiction. Her work has appeared in *The Coachella Review,Elohi Gadugi, Mount Island, Vine Leaves, Section 8, The Pitkin Review*, and *Beyond Parallax*.

Emily Koon is a fiction writer from North Carolina. She has work in *Potomac Review, The Rumpus, Portland Review* and other places. She can be found at twitter.com/thebookdress.

Maryse Meijer's work has appeared in *Joyland, Meridian, The Dallas Review, The Portland Review, St. Ann's Review, 580 Split,* and elsewhere. Her collection of stories, *Heartbreaker*, was published by FSG as part of their Paperback Originals series.

[contributor bios]

Jessica Roeder lives in Duluth, Minnesota, where she teaches writing and dance. Her work has appeared in *Threepenny Review*, *Third Coast*, *American Poetry Review*, and elsewhere. She has received a Pushcart Prize and a McKnight Artist Fellowship.

Originally from Buffalo, New York, **Jasmine Sawers** now lives and writes in Lexington, Kentucky.

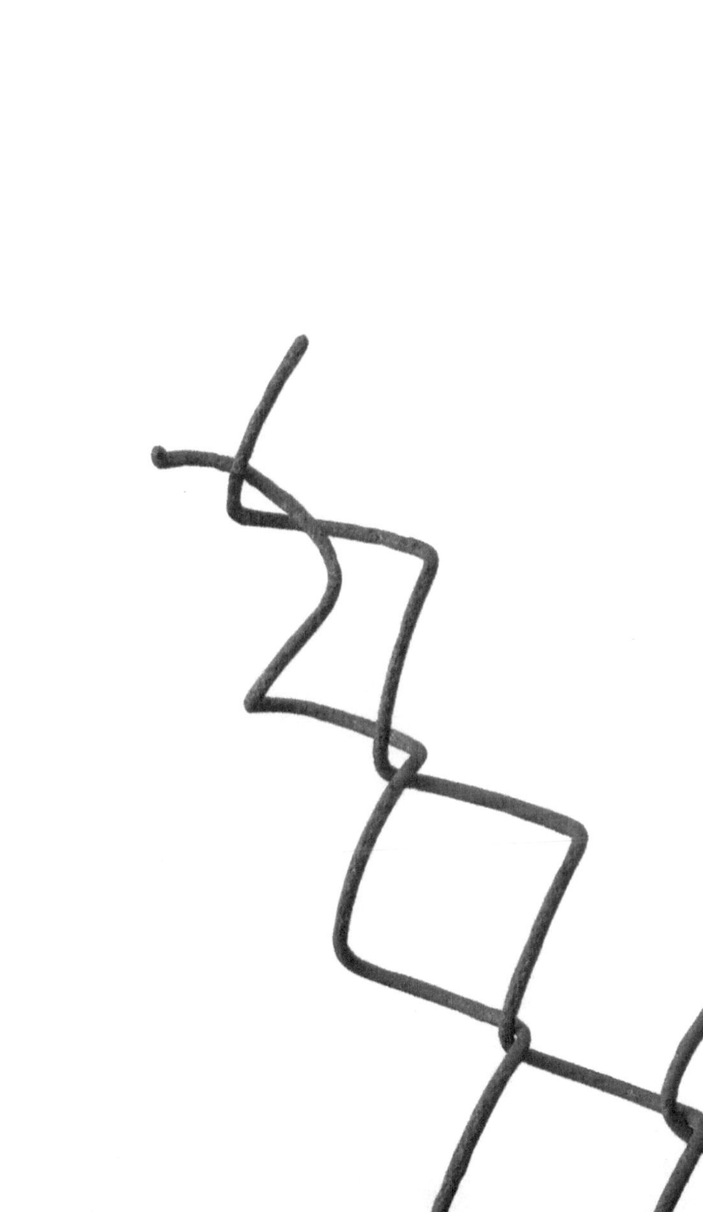